HOW TO TIE A SHOE

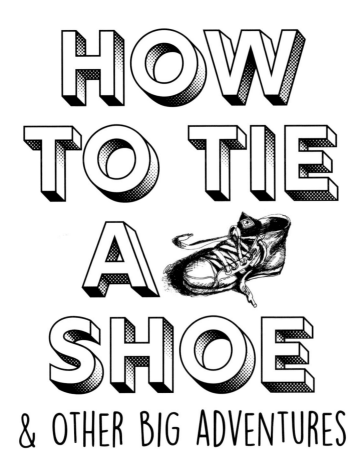

& OTHER BIG ADVENTURES

ILLUSTRATED BY **SKIP HILL**

penny candy BOOKS

Penny Candy Books
Oklahoma City & Greensboro

Text © 2020 Penny Candy Books
Illustrations & photo of Skip Hill © 2020 Skip Hill

 This book is printed on paper certified to the environmental and social standards of the Forest Stewardship Council™ (FSC®).

Design: Shanna Compton

24 23 22 21 20   1 2 3 4 5
ISBN-13: 978-0-9996584-8-2 (hardcover)

Small press. Big conversations.
www.pennycandybooks.com

If you've ever eaten spaghetti

PASTA KING
TRY OUR
SALE
BA
GARDE

CHEESE

or pointed out
a bird's nest
to a friend
in spring

OR COMBED your hair after sleeping hard on your head

First, you put
your hands in front
of you, and then

you
forget about them
for a second.

Think instead about how you used to TRACE your fingers across the patterns on rugs in your Grandparents' house.

Think about getting LOST IN the woods and finding your WAY BACK again using ONLY the sounds of bIRDS as A guide

Think about reALizing slowly, slowly, then suddenly, that you're AWAKE

and the
whole day lies
tangled before you
Like a knot.

Now
remember
your hands.

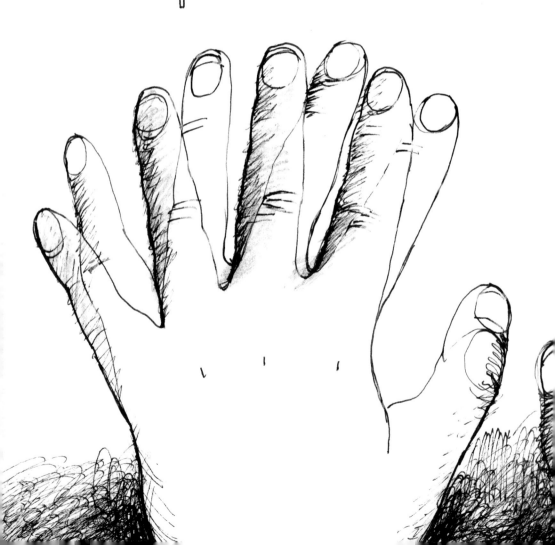

Wiggle your fingers. See the half moons in your nails?

Like a shy friend coming back to school after SUMMER BREAK?

That feeling of seeing Her again for the first time, and the feeling of her seeing YOU

and
the TWO
of you
hugging

and all
the words happening
at once, and everything
coming untangled
and tied

COOKiE PiCKLE
SNAP

BUBBLE
GUM

WOOT
WOOT?

HOME
RUN

BINGO

and you're
feeling snug and tight
Like you could RUN
a million miles?

SH!
A
KNOCK
KNOCK
YOU
AH! CAN DO THIS
OH YEAH!

That's how you
tie a shoe.

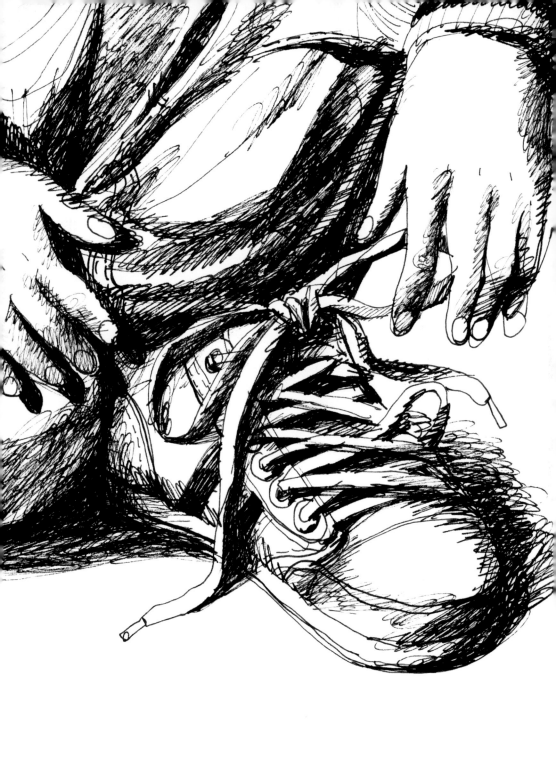

Skip Hill is a mixed-media visual artist whose art is in private and public collections throughout the US, Europe, and Latin America. He is the illustrator of the picture book *A Gift from Greensboro* (Penny Candy Books, 2016) by poet Quraysh Ali Lansana. Skip is also one of thirteen illustrators who contributed work to *Thirteen Ways of Looking at a Black Boy* (Penny Candy Books, 2018) by Tony Medina. Skip lives in Tulsa, OK.